Hang-ten with some way-rad rhinos as they shoot the tube!

Brilliantly colored watercolor illustrations bring the thrills and spills of surfing alive as three radical rhinos take to the waves. The playful text, complete with a glossary of surfing lingo, is perfect for reading aloud, and the way-cool pictures make sharing this book a totally awesome reading experience.

"Mammano's delightful offering will have readers smiling from cover to cover as rhinos ride the waves. . . . Children who have watched surfers from the shore will be pleased to find a book about this subject, while those inland will appreciate its sheer fun and buoyant exuberance."
—★*School Library Journal,* starred review

"With curving, twirling lines, bright watercolors, and soft, complex, often geometric designs, this picture book is a visual delight."
—*Parents' Choice,* Honors Award Recipient

To my parents, Louis and Judith Mammano, with love and
appreciation which goes beyond words.

First paperback edition published in 2006 by Chronicle Books LLC.

Book design by Lucy Nielsen.
Typeset in Gills Sans Ultra.
Manufactured in Hong Kong.
ISBN-10 0-8118-5229-6
ISBN-13 978-0-8118-5229-6

The Library of Congress has catalogued the previous edition
as follows:
Rhinos who surf / Julie Mammano.
Summary: Rhinos who surf get up early, paddle out, and have fun
until the sun goes down when they ride the last wave to shore.
Includes surfer lingo and a glossary of terms.
ISBN: 0-8118-1000-3 (hc)
[1. Surfing—Fiction. 2. Rhinoceroses—Fiction.] I. Title.
PZ7.M3117Rh 1996   95-38240
[E]—dc20   CIP
AC

Distributed in Canada by Raincoast Books
9050 Shaughnessy Street, Vancouver, British Columbia V6P 6E5

10 9 8 7 6 5 4 3 2 1

Chronicle Books LLC
85 Second Street, San Francisco, California 94105

www.chroniclekids.com

Rhinos Who Surf

BY JULIE MAMMANO

chronicle books · san francisco

Rhinos who surf get up early.

They grab their
BOARDS . . .

...and hop in the car.

They **WAX** their boards.

They PADDLE out.

Rhinos who surf have no fear of **MONDO** waves.

They **CARVE UP THE FACE.**

They GO VERTICAL

and SLAM THE LIP.

They pull **KILLER AERIALS.**

When they SHOOT THE TUBE, they are WAY COOL in the GREEN ROOM.

They are **PITCHED** over the **FALLS.**

They are **LAUNCHED** through the air.

Surf Lingo

Aerial   a surfing move done in the air

Amped   really happy

Awesome   great

Bail   jump off a surfboard to avoid an accident

Boards   surfboards

Carve up   do lots of skillful moves on a wave

Cool   really good

Drop in   slide from the top of a wave to the bottom

Dweebs   jerks who surf

Excellent   great

Face   the big blue part of the wave

Falls   the crashing part of a wave that forms a waterfall

Full-on   very

Fully   very

Go vertical   make a sharp upward movement on a wave

Gnarly   bad, scary

Green room   the space inside a tube wave

Jam   go really fast

Killer   really great

Launched   be thrown in the air (usually from a *gnarly wipe out*)

Major   very

Mondo   very big

Paddle   move your arms through the water, like an oar, to propel the surfboard

Pitched   be thrown in the air

Pumping   (waves) coming in one after another

Rinse cycle   the choppy, churning water from a crashing wave

Shoot the tube   surf through the tube

Shred   surf really well

Slam the lip   hit the top of a wave as it starts to curl over

Snake   steal someone else's wave

Tasty   really great

Thrashed   get tumbled around in the water

Totally   very

Tube   a wave that forms a tube or pipe shape

Wax   sticky stuff that makes a surfer's feet stay on the board

Way   very

Wipe-out   a fall or a crash

Julie Mammano, born and raised in Southern California, began surfing as an adult. This book was inspired by her surfing experiences. (She was waiting for the next wave when she got the idea.) Julie is now a freelance artist and illustrator who works and surfs in Southern California.

Also by Julie Mammano

Rhinos Who Snowboard
Rhinos Who Skateboard
Rhinos Who Play Soccer
Rhinos Who Play Baseball